PIN THE TAIL ON THE DONKEY

Pin the Tail on the Donkey

and other party games

Compiled by **Joanna Cole**
and **Stephanie Calmenson**

illustrated by **Alan Tiegreen**

chronicle books · san francisco

First Chronicle Books LLC edition published in 2004.

Manufactured in Hong Kong.

ISBN 1-58717-229-1

Library of Congress Cataloging-in-Publication Data available.

Distributed in Canada by Raincoast Books
9050 Shaughnessy Street
Vancouver, British Columbia V6P 6E5

10 9 8 7 6 5 4 3 2 1

Chronicle Books LLC
85 Second Street
San Francisco, California 94105

www.chroniclekids.com

CONTENTS

PARTY GAMES FOR YOUNG CHILDREN

You have a birthday child and a house full of friends, all ready to have fun. It's time for some party games!

The games in this book are designed for young party-goers from four-years-old to about seven or eight. The games are simple and fun, and they are noncompetitive, because younger children love games but are not usually ready for winning and losing.

For this age group, the fun of games is simply in the playing. So while rules are important, it helps to have an adult leader who will bend the rules every now and then. This may mean guiding a child a little closer to the goal in a throwing game such as "Feed the Monster," becoming a low-key partner with a child who's having trouble finding peanuts in "Peanut Hunt," or giving a slowpoke some extra steps in "Giant Steps."

Of course, when children get together in one place, they are bound to get boisterous. It helps to alternate some action games with some quiet ones. For instance, after playing "Jack Be Nimble" and "Musical Chairs," calm things down with "Let's Go Apple Picking" or "Telephone."

Deciding who goes first is important to children. For the first game or two, the birthday child may go first. Then he or she may choose someone to begin, who then chooses the next player. Or you may want to let children draw numbers from a hat or box, which is fun in itself.

Always keep safety in mind. If games are played indoors, remind children to *walk*, not run. Avoid party favors with sharp edges, and remember that for toddlers, small toys or toys with small parts are a choking hazard, as are deflated or broken balloons and foods such as hard candies, grapes, and hot dogs.

In this book there are step-by-step instructions, plenty of pictures, and a sprinkling of hints throughout. We hope it will help make your child's next party a success!

PIN THE TAIL ON THE DONKEY

You will need:

- picture of a donkey without a tail

- paper tails with a child's name on each

- tape for each tail (no pins needed!)

- blindfold

1. Blindfold the first child.

2. Slowly turn her three times.

3. Give her a tail.

4. Point her in the right direction.

5. Repeat with each child.

6. When all the tails are on, clap for all the funny places they landed.

For variety:
Play "Stick the Nose on the Clown," "Put the Tail on the Dinosaur," "Put the Tire on the Truck," etc.

For older children:
The child whose tail is closest to the right place is the winner.

CATCH THAT BALLOON!

You will need:
- a balloon

1. Have children gather around you.

2. Toss balloon in the air and call one child's name.

3. That child tries to catch the balloon before it touches the ground.

4. If the child succeeds, he gets to toss the balloon and call the next name.

△ ▽ △

For very young children:
An adult should toss and call the whole game.

Safety tip:
Always supervise young children around balloons. A broken balloon is a choking hazard.

▽ △ ▽

FEED THE MONSTER

1. Everyone takes a turn tossing three items of "food" into the monster's mouth.

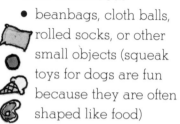

2. After each child's turn, retrieve the "food" and hand it to the next child.

3. Every time a child "feeds" the monster, he gets a prize: Put a sticker on his shirt!

— 13 —

Helpful hint:
If children have trouble getting the food into the mouth, let them stand a little closer.

JACK, OR JILL, BE NIMBLE

You will need:

- a wooden block

1. Place the block on the floor toward one end of the room.

2. Children line up at the other end.

3. One at a time, the children jump over the block while everyone recites, "Jill be nimble, Jill be quick, Jill jump over the candlestick."

For older children:
Pile on more blocks. Children who knock over the blocks are out. The child who jumps over the most blocks wins.

DRAW-A-FACE RELAY

1. Children form teams of about five players and stand in line across the room from the papers.

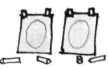

2. On the word "Go," the first child on each team must *walk* to a paper and draw the eyes on the face.

3. When she is finished, she walks back to her team.

4. The next child walks to the paper and draws a nose.

5. Team members continue walking and drawing the mouth, ears, and hair.

6. The first team to have eyes, ears, nose, mouth, and hair wins.

LIMBO

You will need:
- a long pole, mop, or broomstick

- piano or tape player (Caribbean music, if possible)

1. Two adults hold the pole at child height.

2. Start the music. Children must walk under the pole without touching it.

3. After each round, the adults lower the pole an inch or two.

4. When the pole gets very low, children may bend backward and shimmy under, or they may crawl.

5. If a player touches the pole, she is out.

DO THE CONGA!

1. Everyone forms a line with hands on the hips of the person in front.

2. Everybody sings "Do the Conga" and dances forward.

DO THE CONGA!

Ev-'ry-bod-y Con-ga!_ Come and do the Con-ga!_

4. On the next "Conga," everyone puts the left foot out, and so on.

3. On the first "Conga," the line stops and everyone puts the right foot out.

5. You can dance all over the house, even outside!

Ev - 'ry-bod - y Con - ga!_ Do the Con - ga now!

MUSICAL CHAIRS

You will need:

- straight chairs (one *less* than the number of children)

- piano or tape player

1. Set up chairs in a row, with adjacent chairs facing the opposite way.

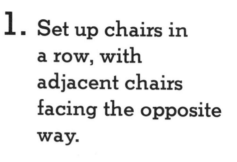

2. When the music starts, the children walk around the chairs in a circle.

— 22 —

3. When the music stops, the children sit down. One child will be left standing.

4. Start the music and the game again—with everybody playing.

△ ▽ △

For older children:
Take away one chair after each round. The players who are out move to the side. The child who gets the last chair is the winner.

▽ △ ▽

FOLLOW THE LEADER

1. The birthday child gets to be the leader. Everyone forms a line behind him.

2. The children follow the leader as he marches, hops, skips, taps his head, etc.

3. When the adult signals (by ringing a bell or calling out "Change!"), the leader goes to the end of the line, and the next child becomes the leader.

4. Repeat until everyone has had a turn.

SIMON SAYS

1. Children stand in a group in front of the leader.

2. The leader says, "Simon says, 'Do this,'" as she taps her head, claps her hands, turns around, etc.

3. The children must follow the leader's actions, but *only* if she begins with "Simon says..."

4. If the leader just says "Do this," the children must do nothing.

△ ▽ △

For older children:
If a child makes a mistake,
he is out. The last child
"in" is the winner.

▽ △ ▽

 **GIANT STEPS**

1. Children stand in a row against the wall at one end of the room.

2. The leader stands at the other end and calls a child by name, saying, for example, "Mary, you may take three baby steps." The number and type of steps can vary with each child.

3. Mary *must* say, "May I?" If she does not, her turn is over.

△ ▽ △

Helpful hint:
Here are some typical steps: giant, baby, hops, twirls, jumps, backward, and tiptoes. Or make up funny ones such as duck waddles or skater slides.

▽ △ ▽

4. If the leader says, "Yes, you may," Mary then takes three baby steps toward the leader.

5. If the leader says, "No, you may not," Mar must stay put. The leader may also change the number or type of steps: "No, you may not. You may take two giant steps."

6. Mary must remember to say "May I?" again. If she does not, she must go back to the wall.

7. The first child to reach the leader wins.

JACK-IN-THE-BOX

You will need:
- paper badges with the numerals 1 and 2

- tape to stick badges on children's shirts

1. The children sit on the floor, and each child pretends to be a jack-in-the-box.

2. Assign children to two teams by taping a badge to each child. Each child must remember if he is a "1" or a "2."

3. An adult claps once. All the 1's must jump up.

4. When the leader claps twice, the 2's jump up.

5. When the leader claps three times, *all* the children jump up.

6. Whoever jumps up on the wrong number has to stand on one leg and hop in place while turning around before sitting down again.

PEANUT HUNT

1. Each child gets a bag.

You will need:
- peanuts (in their shells)

- paper bags

Before the party:
- Hide peanuts all around the room.

2. An adult gives the signal (rings a bell, blows a horn, etc.), and the hunt begins.

3. Children look for peanuts and fill up their bags.

4. When no more peanuts can be found, the children have fun counting their peanuts.

For older children: The child who has the most peanuts is the winner.

FISH FOR A SURPRISE

You will need:
- small party favors or treats

- gift wrap and ribbon

- stick or ruler

- string
- metal paper clip

Before the party:
- Wrap each treat. (Make sure the bows have *big* loops.)

- Make a fishing pole with a stick, string, and paper-clip hook.

Easier for you:
Just tie ribbons around any small objects and call the game "Fishing for Fun."

1. Place presents in a laundry basket, small plastic swimming pool, or on the floor.

2. Everyone gets a turn fishing for a present.

 # HOT AND COLD

You will need:
- a small object such as a child's toy

1. One child is "It." He leaves the room while the others hide the object.

2. "It" comes back and looks for the object.

3. When "It" gets close, the others say, "You are getting warm (warmer...hot!)."

4. When "It" moves away from the object, they say, "You are getting cold (colder...freezing!)."

5. The children keep helping until "It" finds the object. Then another child goes out, and the game begins again.

LET'S GO APPLE PICKING!

You will need:
- a tub of water
- an apple (with a stem) for each child
- a small gift or treat for each child
- gift wrap
- colored ribbons
- blindfold

Before the party:
- Wrap gifts, using a different color ribbon for each one.
- Tie a bow on each apple stem (a different color for each apple).

1. Blindfold the first child and let another child lead her to the tub.

2. All the children chant: "Green, pink, yellow, blue, Which apple is for you?"

3. The child picks an apple from the tub and takes off the blindfold.

4. Then the child may take a gift with the same color ribbon.

5. When everyone has had a turn, children open their gifts and eat their apples.

Easier for you:
Put the apples on a table or in a basket instead of a tub of water.

PASS THE PACKAGE

You will need:

- small treats (candies or raisins)

- gift wrap
- tape

- piano or tape player

Before the party:

- Wrap one treat.

- Wrap the package *and* another treat.

- Wrap the second package *and* another treat.

- Do this until you have a big package with a treat for each child.

2. Stop the music. The child who has the package unwraps one layer and eats the treat.

1. Start the music. Children pass the package around the circle.

3. Start the music again. Keep playing until each child gets a treat.

4. Keep track of who has already gotten a treat. Make sure everyone gets one by turning off the music at the appropriate time.

△ ▽ △

Easier for you:
Put treats in a bag. When the music stops, the child may reach in and take one.

▽ △ ▽

TELEPHONE

1. Children sit in a circle.

2. An adult whispers a phrase or sentence in one child's ear.

3. That child whispers what he heard to the next child.

4. That child whispers what she heard...and so on.

5. The last child says aloud what he heard. It will be very different from the original!

△ ▽ △

Helpful hint:
Here are some suggestions for telephone sentences:
- Here comes the merry mermaid.
- Whistle while you work.
- Can you scoop strawberry ice cream?
- It's raining cats and dogs.

▽ △ ▽

HA! HA! HA!

1. Everyone sits in a circle.

2. One child says, "HA!"

3. The next child adds a second "**HA!**" saying, "**HA! HA!**"

4. The third child adds another "**HA!**" saying, "**HA! HA! HA!**"... and so on.

5. The object of the game is to keep a straight face.

For older children: Have each child lie down, resting his or her head on the stomach of the next child. The last child to laugh is the winner.

 # DUCK, DUCK, GOOSE!

1. Children sit in a circle. One child is "It" and walks around the outside of the circle.

2. "It" taps each child lightly on the head and says, "Duck…"

3. At any time, "It" may tap a child and call out "Goose" instead of "Duck." The "Goose" jumps up and chases "It" around the circle.

4. "Goose" must try to tag "It" before "It" sits in "Goose's" empty place. If "It" is tagged, he is "It" again. If "It" is not tagged, then "Goose" becomes "It."

For variety:
Instead of saying "Duck, Duck, Goose," try the game as "Cat, Cat, Dog," or even, "Happy, Happy, Birthday."

WHERE TO FIND MORE

SOME SOURCES FOR PARTY GAMES

52 Fun Party Activities for Kids by Lynn Gordon. Chronicle Books LLC, 1996.

365 TV-Free Activities You Can Do with Your Child by Steve and Ruth Bennett. Adams Media, third edition, 2002.

Birthday Parties: Best Party Tips & Ideas by Vicki Lansky. The Book Peddlers, third edition, 2003.

Einstein's Science Parties: Easy Parties for Curious Kids by Shar Levine and Allison Grafton. John Wiley & Son, 1994.

Hopscotch, Hangman, Hot Potato, and Ha, Ha, Ha: A Rulebook of Children's Games by Jack Maguire. Fireside, 1992.

I Can Have a Party!: Party Activity Projects for Children by Thomasina Smith. Lorenz Books, 2000.

Kids' Party Games and Activities: Hundreds of Exciting Things to Do at Parties for Kids 2-12 by Penny Warner, illustrations by Kathy Rogers. Aladdin Library, 1993.

Kids' Outdoor Parties, by Penny Warner, illustrations by Connelly Gwen. Meadowbrook, 1999.

Party Secrets: Who to Invite, Must-Dance Music, Most-Loved Munchies & Foolproof Fun! by Sarah Jane Brian, illustrations by Debra Dixon. Pleasant Company Publications, 2003.

The Star Wars Party Book: Recipes and Ideas for Galactic Occasions by Mikyla Bruder, photographs by Frankie Frankeny. Chronicle Books LLC, 2002.